John Johnston

Musa Medica

A Sheaf of Song and Verse

John Johnston

Musa Medica
A Sheaf of Song and Verse

ISBN/EAN: 9783337179533

Printed in Europe, USA, Canada, Australia, Japan

Cover: Foto ©Andreas Hilbeck / pixelio.de

More available books at **www.hansebooks.com**

MUSA · MEDICA:

A SHEAF

OF

SONG AND VERSE.

BY

J. JOHNSTON, M.D., EDIN.

London:

THE SAVOY PRESS, LTD., SAVOY HOUSE, 115, STRAND, W.C

1897.

Price, 2s. 6d.

THE SAVOY PRESS, LTD.,
SAVOY HOUSE, 115, STRAND, W.C.

CONTENTS.

Nature, and Local Songs and Verses—*cont.*

Other Songs and Verses—

TO

THE MASTER

AND THE BOYS OF

THE EAGLE STREET COLLEGE,

FROM WHOM SO MANY OF THESE

SONGS AND VERSES RECEIVED THEIR INITIAL

IMPULSE, THIS LITTLE VOLUME

IS AFFECTIONATELY

DEDICATED

BY

THE AUTHOR.

Bolton, 1897.

The Song of the Eagle Street College.*

1.

Did ye ever hear tell ov the Aegle Strate School,
An' the rale dacint Boys that go there, as a rule?
Thin light up yer pipe an' draw in yer stool,
   While I sing yez the Song ov our College.
The tachin' at Aegle Strate's far an' away
The best in the wurruld—at laste so the Boys say ;
An' the best ov it is that there's nothin' to pay
   For the larnin' at Aegle Strate College.

Chorus.—Och, Boys! We're the Pheelosiphers !
   We are the wans for the Knowledge !
   Av ye want Eddication,
   Or correct Information,
   Come an' jine the Aegle Strate College.

---

* "*Eagle Street College*" *is the name given to a group of friends in Bolton.*

II.

The Masther himself is a wonderful man ;

Shure, he's read all the clever folk's books wan by
    wan,

An' there's nothin' on earth he does not undershtan';

    There's no tellin' the depth ov his knowledge.

By the Boys he is held in the heighth ov estame,

An' 'tis mighty small wonder that he is that same—

For doesn't he shtan' them all cocoa an' crame

    Every Monday night at the College ?

    Chorus.—Och, Boys ! We're the Pheelosiphers !

        We are the wans for the Knowledge !

        Av ye're wantin' Theology,

        Or Anthropology,

        Come an' jine the Aegle Strate College.

III.

The Scholars for ignorance nothin' can bate,

Though ov coorse *they* consider their larnin' is great;

What they're short ov in larnin's made up in consate,

    Wid the Boys ov the Aegle Strate College.

There's a "Blackin'-hole" Boy who thinks he can

      paint,

An' when he's drest up ye might think he's a saint;

But don't be desaived!   For that's *not* the complaint

    Ov that Boy at the Aegle Strate College.

      Chorus.—Och, Boys! We're the Pheelosiphers!

        We are the wans for the Knowledge!

          Av yer laenin's artistic,

          Or rationalistic,

        Come an' jine the Aegle Strate College.

IV.

Then wan ov them Boys is a Limb ov the Law,
Ov ould Epictaetus he'd kape us in awe,
An' he says, anny minute he's ready to draw
    The wills ov the Boys at the College.
The next Boy may be known by the yarn on his
    clothes;
He's as good as a mother, as every wan knows,
Shure, he mends all the stockin's an' knits all the hose
    Ov the Boys at the Aegle Strate College.

    Chorus.—Och, Boys! We're the Pheelosiphers!
        We are the wans for the Knowledge!
          Av ye want laegal larnin'
          Or yer stockin's nade darnin',
        Come an' jine the Aegle Strate College.

V.

To larn all about African travellers, shure,

Ye'd better get thick wid the Sage ov Tonge Moor;

The jaynius is great, but the pay's mighty poor

    Ov the ex-newspaper Boy at the College.

Wan takes care ov their money—but I'd better explain

When they ax for it back, shure, their axin's in vain;

For begorra, they never set eyes on't again

    When it's banked wid this Boy at the College.

Chorus.—Och, Boys! We're the Pheelosiphers!

    We are the wans for the Knowledge!

    Av ye've got anny money,

    We'll look after it, sonny,

    Av ye'll jine the Aegle Strate College.

VI.

A Clargyman's name on the school roll appairs,

But *he* doesn't give himself clargyman airs ;

An' he takes a dape interest in the affairs

 That consarn the Boys at the College.

He's a good-hearted fellow, an' ov praise has no

  nade ;

He's a prince among parsons ov every crade ;

He can joke an' can smoke the delectable wade,

 Like the rest ov the Boys at the College.

  Chorus.—Och, Boys ! We're the Pheelosiphers !

   We are the wans for the Knowledge !

    For Christian tachin',

    Widout dogmatic prachin',

   Come an' jine the Aegle Strate College.

VII.

Another wan sports an M.D. ov his own,

Which his long-sufferin' patients say manes 'money
down';

Wid this licence to murther, shure, he's kilt half the
town,

But they won't let him practhice in College.

There's an Architect Boy who's as round as a praist;

That he's fond ov his dinner ye may tell by his waist;

Though the last on the list he's by no manes the laste,

Ov the Boys ov the Aegle Strate College.

Chorus.—Och, Boys! We're the Pheelosiphers!

We are the wans for the Knowledge!

Av ye want Architecture,

Or may be a Health Lecture,

Ye must come to the Aegle Strate

College.

B

VIII.

There's wan other gintleman's name to be towld,

Whom we're proud to call *friend*, av we may be so
　　bowld,—

'Tis our Visitor here, whose heart ov rale gowld

　　Is well known to the Boys ov the College.

The Talks ov the Boys are varied an' free ;

From　Brownin'　an'　Whitman　to　a　Parish　Church
　　spree—

For, be jabers, there's mortial few things won't agree

　　Wid the Boys ov the Aegle Strate College.

　　　　Chorus.—Och, Boys !　We're the Pheelosiphers !

　　　　　　　　We are the wans for Knowledge !

　　　　　　　　　Av ye want to larn Science

　　　　　　　　　An' bid Huxley defiance,

　　　　　　　Come an' jine the Aegle Strate College.

IX.

The lessons them Boys have to larn are sevare,
An' manny's the time they feel tempted to swear—
But sorra a ha'p'orth the Masther 'ud care
    For the threats ov the Boys at the College.
He tells them if ever they wish to be *men*,
They must *practice* them lessons agin an' agin,
Till the wurruld can see for itself that they've been
    Able pupils ov Aegle Strate College.

Chorus.—Och, Boys ! We're the Pheelosiphers !
        We are the wans for the Knowledge !
            Av ye're wanting in Charity.—
            'Mong vartues a rarity—
        Come an' jine the Aegle Strate College.

X.

The love ov the Boys for aich other's sinsare,
While their kind-hearted Masther they almost revare :
An' av anny wan doubts it, he'd better take care
    Ov the fists ov the Boys at the College !
Then long life to the Boys at the Aegle Strate School !
Over them may their well-beloved Masther long rule !
An' may the warm feelin's ov friendship ne'er cool
    'Mong the Boys ov the Aegle Strate College !

     Chorus.—Och, Boys !   We're the Pheelosiphers !
        We are the wans for the Knowledge !
        For the best sart ov Larnin'—
        I'd have yez take warnin'—
        Ye must come to the Aegle Strate
        College.

Bolton, April 29th, 1889.

MEDICAL SONGS AND VERSES.

The Doctor.

Who hourly is at beck and call

Of rich and poor, of great and small ?

Who does his best for each, for all ?

                The Doctor.

Who's welcomed warmly everywhere,

By stalwart men and ladies fair ?

Who to the children all is dear ?

                The Doctor.

Whose toil ends not with close of day ?

Who works while others sleep or play,

And oft plods home in morning grey ?

                The Doctor.

Of politics who takes small heed,

And cares not *what* the patient's creed,

His sole concern—a sick man's need ?

The Doctor.

Who is entrusted with the lives

Of fathers, husbands, mothers, wives ;

And who untiring service gives ?

The Doctor.

Who knows our strength and weakness best,

And holds inviolate in his breast

Our secrets—e'en those unconfessed ?

The Doctor.

Who is the faithful, trusty friend,

On whose help loyal we depend

From life's first dawning to its end ?

The Doctor.

Doctor Air.

Of doctors and their theories of Medicine there's no
lack ;

From knighted court physician to perambulating quack,

There are specialists for everything the human frame
contains,

Between our soles and skull-caps, from our digits to our
brains.

We have Homœopaths, and Allopaths, and Hydropaths,
as well

As Mesmerists—though these are now called Hypnotists
—who'll quell

Neuralgias and all aches and pains, with a mystic
    " pass " or two ;
While the cures of the Faith-healers are most mar-
    vellous—if true.

There's Dr. Blister, Dr. Bleed, and old-fashioned Dr.
    Pill,
Who with his mixtures, potions, draughts will cure your
    every ill ;
And Dr. Sanitation will with wonder make you stare ;
But the king of all the doctors, new or old, is Dr. Air.

He boasts no long, imposing string of letters to his name,
No *Alma Mater* has inscribed him on its roll of fame ;
No walls his consultation room enclose from the blue sky,
Its floor's the broad expanding earth, its roof heaven's
    canopy.

No nauseous drugs does he prescribe our illnesses to
    cure,

His medicine's elemental, tonic, wholesome, sweet and
  pure ;
His services professional to each and all are free—
For Nature's own physician ne'er exacts reward nor fee.

No horse nor carriage he requires, he neither walks nor
  rides,
But floats on pinions vaporous, from woods and green
  hill-sides,
Where golden sunbeams glint and dance among the
  pretty flowers,
To the music of clear purling brooks and birds in leafy
  bowers.

He voyages across the sea, whose breath ozonic clings
About his vesture as he flies, with healing on his wings.
For men and women stricken sore by dire disease or
  pain
He bears the balm that's sanative and bringeth back
  again

The roses to the pallid cheek, the sparkle to the eye,

Infusing strength—nay, life itself—in sick humanity.

What purblind folly 'tis for men to poison and pollute

This true *elixir vitæ* with their chemicals and soot !

Transforming heaven's own ether pure into mephitic
gas,

Destroying precious health and blighting trees and
flowers and grass.

How long will Mammon worshippers befoul our precious
store

Of vitalizing oxygen and 'gainst it shut their door ?

By oxygen we live and move, deprived of it we die :

Thus is the life of Earth-born man related to the Sky.

Then who would healthy, happy be, must daily have a
care

To quaff a copious draught from life-inspiring Dr. Air.

The General Practitioner.—*A Song.*

Come, friends, who to the Medical Society belong,

And give me your attention while I sing a little song :

It's all about the troubles and the trials that befall

The General Practitioner in his life professional.

His first and foremost trouble is that patients stay away,

But soon he finds a greater when their bills they will
  not pay ;

For he's not long discovering, when he has done his
  work,

That a patient thinks it no great shame the doctor's bill
  to shirk.

He must not walk his rounds for fear his patients think
 him poor ;
And dearly do they love to see a carriage at their door.
If his horse is fat, they say—" he must have little work
 to do,"
And if it's lean, the reason is —" he starves the poor old
 screw."

If he often goes to Church, folks say—" it's all hypocrisy,"
And if he doesn't go at all—" an Atheist he must be ; "
And when he is called out, as down the aisle he passes by,
The knowing ones exchange a look and wink the other
 eye.

About money he must always seem indifferent to be,
And folks may think he practises from pure philanthropy.
When we hear about him boasting of the guineas that
 he earns,
We wonder if they all appear in his income-tax returns.

He must work all day, and half the night, and never say

    he's tired ;

For the public look upon him simply as a servant hired :

And should he take a holiday, he'll find, when he comes

    back,

Some patients have resented it by giving him " the

    sack."

Should he call upon his patients every day when they

    are ill,

His motive plainly is—" to make a great big doctor's

    bill :"

If he visits them less frequently—thus lessening their

    expense—

The chances are he'll be accused of wilful negligence.

The most grateful creature on the earth is a patient—

    while he's ill ;

But his feelings sometimes alter when he gets the doctor's

    bill ;

And the doctor thus can judge how much the gratitude
    is worth,

When he sees it taking flight with the disease that gave
    it birth.

Oh, it's fine to be a doctor, for his work is only play !

He has nothing else to do but in a carriage ride all day :

To say nothing of the pleasure and the unalloyed
    delight

He always feels when patients call him out of bed at
    night.

About his own afflictions he must never say a word—

The idea of a doctor ill, is really so absurd !

And when, perhaps from overwork, he's laid upon the
    shelf,

His sympathising patients say—" Physician, heal thy-
    self ! "

Sung at the Annual Dinner of the Bolton and District Medical
Society, October 4th, 1894.

The Young Medico.—*A Song.*

If Medicine is the line in which you wish to shine

    As a popular G.P.,

There are certain things which you must not forget to do,

    If successful you would be.

Real talent doesn't matter, so long as you can smatter

    About things that are taught at College,

And give folks to understand that you have at your command

    Unlimited stores of knowledge ;

        And everyone will say,

        As you walk your medical way—

" If this young man is as wise as he looks, with his L.R.C.P.E.,

Why, what a very wise young medico this medico must be !"

When you're called into a case you must wear a solemn
　　　face,
　　　And pronounce it serious ;
No matter whether it is a catarrh or meningitis,
　　　And the patient delirious ;
The result is sure to raise you, and the friends are sur
　　　to praise you,
　　　For your penetration great ;
Should the patient not recover, the reason they'll discove
　　　Is that *you* have been called too late.
　　　　　And everyone will say,
　　　　　As you walk your infallible way—
" If this young man displays such great professi
　　　ability,
Why, what a very clever young medico this medico
　　　must be ! "

You must cultivate the arts that captivate the hearts
    Of the ladies one and all,
And before your person neat and your manners suave
      and sweet,
    They at your feet will fall ;
Your directions they will follow, and your physic they
      will swallow,
    Whenever they are taken ill ;
They'll smile and bow around you, at assemblies they'll
      surround you,
    And your surgery they'll fill.
      And everyone will say,
      When they see your taking way—
" If this young man is so popular 'mong the ladies in
      Society,
Why, what a very nice young medico this medico must
      be !"

In obedience to your rules, you'll call other doctors
  fools,
  Whether they be old or young,
And of course insinuate that their treatment's out of
  date,
  And their diagnosis wrong.
The fact that you're cut dead by every other *med*,
  With contemptuous indifference you'll view :
So your rivalling physician is regarded with suspicion,
  And the patients send for *you.*
    And everyone will say,
    As you walk your triumphant way—
" If this young man speaks so slightingly of his brethren
  of every degree,
Why, what a most superior young medico this medico
  must be !"

And when to church you hie, with becoming gravity,

    You'll sit close to the altar ;

For of course you'll have your pew where you'll be in

    fullest view,

    When responding from your psalter.

When the sermon is half o'er, there's a message at the

    door,

    From a patient who is seriously ill ;

He's in such a dangerous state that he really cannot

    wait,

    And urgently demands your skill.

       And everyone will say,

       As you walk down the aisle that day—

" If this young man is called out of church so very

    frequently,

Why, what a very busy young medico this medico must

    be ! "

You'll grow rich and be respected and one day you'll be
    elected
    As a real Town Councillor,
To look after streets and drains and the gas and water
    mains,
    And display your sanitary lore :
Till at last you get to be an Alderman and a J.P.,
    And sit upon the Bench in state ;
And you even may aspire to rise a little higher,
    And become the Chief Magistrate.
        And everyone will say,
        As you walk your exalted way—
" If this young man has climbed so soon to the top of
    the municipal tree,
What a brilliantly-talented medico this medico must
    be ! "

Sung at the Annual Dinner of the Bolton and District Medical
Society, October 5th, 1893.

The Song of the Medical Assistant.

———

When I obtained my Double Qual., so proud a man
   was I,

I thought that I'd get any post for which I might apply;

Advertisements I answered in the *B.M.J.* galore,

And *Lancet* situations I applied for by the score.

That my demands were modest will, I think, to all be
   clear,

When I say the "screw" I asked was but a hundred
   pounds a year :

But the members of the Medical Profession are so thrifty,

That the salary they offered me was something nearer
   fifty.

With one of these I'm now engaged, and 'tis no sinecure,
So numerous and varied are the troubles I endure ;
My position in the household is a strange anomaly—
For I must not with the servants dine, nor with the
　　　family.

All duties that unpleasant are my Principal will shirk,
And relegates them all to me as " the Assistant's work ; "
I have to bear the brunt of every grumbling man's
　　　assault,
And when anything goes wrong it's always " the
　　　Assistant's fault."

The Doctor does his daily rounds with horse and trap,
　　　but I
Must go on "Shanks's pony," be the weather wet or
　　　dry ;
He sends me to the folks from whom he hopes but little
　　　pelf,
But his wealthy, paying patients are attended by himself.

I visit all the "clubs" and paupers living in the slums,

And mix the physic for each one who to the Surgery

comes ;

I dress the cuts and wounds and sores and on the

patients wait,

I keep the books, make out the bills, draw teeth and

vaccinate.

I've not an hour to call my own, not even when in bed,

For that confounded night-bell rings directly o'er my head;

And often when my Principal fast locked in sleep remains,

I'm yawning by a bed obstetric, waiting for the pains.

The way some patients speak of me would any man

annoy—

They are so free with their remarks about "that beardless

boy,"

And to their friends and neighbours say, in most con-

temptuous vein,

They "really hope the Dr. will not send that lad again."

If there's a creature medical whose life and lot are worse

Than the Medical Assistant it must be the Doctor's
      horse ;

My insults and annoyances I can no longer brook,

So I've made up my mind that soon I'll start on my own
      hook.

Sung at the Annual Dinner of the Bolton and District Medical
Society, October 17th, 1895.

A Patent=Medicine Song.

Come, friends and members of our Medical Society
Assembled round the festive board, and listen unto me,
While I sing about the marv'llous notions, lotions,
    draughts, and pills,
That are guaranteed to cure the human race of all its ills.

Of weakness of the muscles or the nerves, wherever felt,
You'll speedily be cured by wearing an " Electric Belt";
What matter if it's only made of little bits of tin?
It's called *Electric*, and the metal's nicely quilted in.

For heat spots, pimples, boils, and all " disorders of the
    blood,"
Clarke's mixture, with its *Pot: Iod:* can't fail to do you good;
While Mother Siegel's Syrup, with its treacle and its aloes,
Is a priceless remedy for all, from slum to Royal palace.

And should your stomach be upset, or your liver be at
    fault,

The thing that's sure to put you right is a dose of Eno's
    Salt ;

'Tis true a Seidlitz Powder would have much the same
    effect,

But, as it bears no *patent* stamp, what good can you
    expect ?

For rheumatism nothing can excel St. Jacob's Oil,

With its camphor and its turpentine, pure products of
    the soil ;

For sciatica that's chronic, or lumbago in the back,

Get Sequah's Indian chiefs to rub you till you're blue
    and black.

That women folks are fond of pills old Holloway could
    teach 'em,

But nowadays they're more inclined to pin their faith
    to Beecham,

Whose pills they take by handfuls with a confidence
    nothing shocks ;
For don't they know that " Beecham's Pills are worth
    a guinea a box " ?

For crying babes and children we have nostrums by the
    score,
There are " teething powders," " soothing syrups," and
    " mother's friends " galore ;
And while it's true that all such owe their power to
    " sleeping stuff,"
They soothe the restless little dears—and isn't that
    enough ?

And should your hair evince a strong desire from you
    to part,
At once apply the lotion made by Mrs. Allen's art,
And on each bald and barren spot 'twill soon sprout up
    anew,
While silvery locks will speedily regain their youthful hue.

But time would fail to speak of all the wondrous things
    we hear,

And we marvel at the statements that in circulars
    appear—

How " Warner's Cure," for instance, can *cure* anything
    at all,

If it's true that it contains a large amount of alcohol.

In fact, unless you want to die, there seems no room for
    doubt,

That you must swallow every patent medicine that
    comes out ;

And should you find by doing so you've quite destroyed
    your health,

You'll know at least that you've increased the medicine
    vendor's wealth.

Sung at the Annual Dinner of the Bolton and District Medical
Society, October 13th, 1892.

The Sixpenny Doctor.

By my medical brethren I'm shunned everywhere ;
They call me a " knobstick," and worse names, I fear ;
But sorra a ha'p'orth for them do I care ;
    For I am a Sixpenny Docthor.
My noble profession they all say I disgrace,
And that I deserve drummin' out ov the place;
But my Surgery crowd makes them pull a long face,
    And get mad at the Sixpenny Docthor.

    Chorus.—Och, boys ! I'm the chape Physicker !
        I am the popular docthor !
        Av ye're anythin' ailin',
        Or yer health should be failin',
        Just come to the Sixpenny Docthor !

I'm none ov yer quacks, wid their practhices low,

And wurrums in bottles set out in a row;

But the gowld-framed diplomas in my waitin' room show

    That I'm a legitimate docthor.

Though the docthors are constantly runnin' me down,

My practhice is aequalled by few in the town ;

For who for their physic will pay half-a-crown,

    When they know I'm a Sixpenny Docthor ?

    Chorus.—Och, boys ! I'm the chape Physicker! &c.

My gineral practhice, confess it I must,

Is to charge ready money and never give trust—

For patients must wan an' all down wid their dust,

    When they come to the Sixpenny Docthor.

Though I find them in physic, I give yez my word,

That bottles and boxes the fee won't afford,

So I charge those all extry—and though 'tis absurd,

    'Tis the way wid the Sixpenny Docthor.

    Chorus.—Och, boys ! I'm the chape Physicker! &c.

Folks make a mistake av they think they obtain

Such drugs as *Quinine*, *Pot. Iod.*, and *Henbane*;

For I fear such dear medicines might injure the brain

      Of the Patients who come to the Docthor.

So I dose them wid *Gentian* and *Sodæ Bicarb.*,

Mag. Sulph. and *Tinct. Ferri*, *Pot. Nit.* and *Rhubarb*;

While *Quassia*, in chips, is a mighty chape harb,

      Greatly used by the Sixpenny Docthor.

    Chorus.—Och, boys! I'm the chape Physicker! &c.

But the folks that get off for *wan* sixpence are few;

For I find that their various complaints, ould and new,

Nade plasther, or pills, and a powther or two—

      Extrys all wid the Sixpenny Docthor.

Another smart dodge that I frequently play;

When a patient comes in who looks able to pay,

I tell him I'll call at his house the next day—

      And that's a "bob" for the Sixpenny Docthor.

    Chorus.—Och, boys! I'm the chape Physicker! &c.

D

For Medical Ethics I care not a jot;

And as for my brethren, I despise the whole lot;

For they hate me like pison—and why should they not?

　　　For I'm their great rivallin' Docthor.

They're wan and all jealous of my great success,

Which causes them pocket-felt grief and disthress;

And when their own patients they see growin' less,

　　　They could murther the Sixpenny Docthor.

　　　Chorus.—Och, boys! I'm the chape Physicker! &c.

Ye should hear people talk ov the cures that I do!

But, begorra, if some ov them folks only knew

That half ov them's flukes and the others aren't true,

　　　They'd, maybe, think less ov the Docthor.

But wan thing is certain—that mine's the best way

For makin' our " noble profession " to pay;

Av a medico wants to make money, I say—

　　　Let him start as a Sixpenny Docthor.

　　　Chorus.—Och, boys! I'm the chape Physicker! &c.

John Bolton, C.P.*—*A Ballad.*

John Bolton was a member of the L.I.L.E.C.—

The Loyal Independent Lodge of English Chivalry—

Which paid its Doctor for attending members far and
near

The handsome salary, per head, of half-a-crown a year.

Brave Boys !

Chorus.—With a fal-la-la, &c.

One day John on the Doctor called—not feeling very
well—

And from him he " a bottle " got, his malady to quell.

---

* Club Patient.

He took the medicine home, and great was his astonish-
   ment

To find it *minus* colour, odour, taste, and sediment.

                                    Brave Boys!

He tasted, smelled, and shook it up, then showed it to
   his wife ;

" It's now't but watter, John," she said,—" On that
   I'd lay my life."

" By gow theau'rt reet," said John, " that doctor's tryin'
   on some dodge,

But I'll be upsides wi' 'im, for I'll report 'im to the Lodge."

                                    Brave Boys!

" 'Twould nobbut sarve 'im reet and pay 'im eaut," said
   Mrs. B.,

" For t' let 'im see 'e couldn't make a Johnny foo' o' thee."

Accordingly, next " club neet," beaming with importance
   large,

And hot with indignation, Brother Bolton laid his charge.

Brave Boys!

He said it seemed to him to be a very serious matter,

That "'stead o' physic, Dr. Blank 'ad gan 'im nowt but

watter."

" A very serious charge indeed "—the President declared;

And free were the remarks against the Doctor that were

heard.

Brave Boys!

The issue of the Lodge's sapient deliberation

Was that the Doctor be required to give an explanation.

" All right," was his reply, " but first the bottle must

be sealed,

So that the nature of its contents shall not be revealed."

Brave Boys!

Upon the night appointed for the hearing of the case

The Plaintiff and Defendant each took up his proper
place.

The grievance being stated, and the bottle being laid

Upon the table, Dr. Blank was called upon and said:—

Brave Boys !

" If Brother B. believes 'twas only water that he got,

Then he can no objection have to swallow all the lot :

And this I now insist upon, and claim, if it is found

That he declines my challenge, that his charge falls to
the ground."

Brave Boys !

The Doctor's unexpected words caused great alarm and
pain

To Brother B., who dreaded what that bottle *might*
contain ;

But to the Brethren all it seemed a reasonable request,

So Brother B. was ordered to submit unto the test.

Brave Boys

Alas, poor John ! He'd burned his boats and cut off his
retreat ;

Even hesitation now meant ignominious defeat.

So, with a mock courageousness, he raised the glass and
quaffed

The contents of the bottle at a single gulping draught.

Brave Boys !

" Now," said the Doctor, " Grand Imperial, Vice, and
Brothers all,

While waiting for developments next business you may
call."

John sat awhile, but presently uneasy got to feel,

And, pallid-faced, out of the room he was observed to
    steal.

                          Brave Boys !

A Brother who went after him was much surprised to see

That John was busy making re-acquaintance with his tea!

" Eh, Brother ! I am ill," he said, " I'm deein', sure
    enoof :

I'm pisoned, O, I'm pisoned, Pete, wi' that theere
    Doctor's stuff."

                          Brave Boys !

" Why, Brother Bolton," Peter said, " whatever is the
    matter ?

I thowt tha said as Dr. Blank 'ad gan thee nowt but
    watter !"

  I durn't know what 'e's gan me, but I know I'm
    gradley bad ;

O dear, it's comin' on again ; durn't leave me, Peter
  lad !"

                                        Brave Boys !

A sadder and a wiser man, John hied him home to bed ;

And when Pete told his tale, " It sarved 'im reet," the
  Brethren said.

No more complaints our hero made, but wisely took to
  heart

The lesson that he learned from that large dose of *Antim.
  Tart.*

                                        Brave Boys !

Sung at the Annual Dinner of the Bolton and District Medical
Society, October 13th, 1896.

NATURE AND LOCAL SONGS
AND VERSES.

The Song of the Sunbeam.

From molten heart of mighty Sol
    I traverse interstellar space,
And cleave the clouds which wreathe and roll,
    Like vaporous veils, o'er Earth's fair face.

Mine is the power which liberates
    The cold-imprisoned, ice-gyved world ;
And Monarch Winter's frost-locked gates
    By me are wide asunder hurled.

To Nature captive, slumbering deep,
    I whisper soft, in Spring's sweet voice ;
Bidding her wake from her long sleep,
    And with her children all rejoice.

Dispersed by me are Wintry skies,
    And in my train come Summer days ;
For me the flowerets ope their eyes,
    The song birds trill their roundelays.

The soaring skylark's matin hymn,
    The linnet's gush of melody,
The red-breast's song, in twilight dim,
    Their inspiration owe to me.

I bid the sap, long stagnant, rise
    And course, like vegetable blood,
Through ligneous veins and arteries,
    Till bursts to leaf each brown-sheath'd bud.

By subtle alchemy I make
    The wondrous chlorophyllic hues :
And my prismatic beam I break
    To tints which Nature's artists use.

The modest violet's blue is mine,
  And mine the gold the sunflowers wear;
I paint the rose incarnadine,
  And crimson tip the daisy fair.

I weave the blossoms on my loom,
  And hedge and tree with them bedeck;
I give the peach its velvet bloom,
  And ruddy dye the apple's cheek.

I sparkle in the dewdrop's eye,
  I glint on woodland prattling stream;
Upon each leaf that I espy
  I dance, I shine, I flash, I gleam.

All creatures love to romp and play
  In emerald meads, flower-starr'd by me;
And my benignant, welcome ray
  Cheers hearts that oft a-weary be.

The farmer, without aid from me,
　Would plough and sow his fields in vain ;
'Tis I submerge the fertile lea
　With waving seas of golden grain.

The radiant Night Queen's crescent car
　From me receives its silvery light ;
The colours of the Rainbow are
　But borrowed from my palette bright.

The rosy dawn, the sunset sky,
　From me their glories all obtain ;
The whole wide world I beautify,
　From mountain crest to surging main.

Supreme my sway above, below ;
　Mine is the mystic, potent power
Transmutes, by distillation slow,
　The Ocean into cloud and shower.

The Alpine glacier vast and hoar,
   The iceberg in the Polar sea,
The avalanche with thunderous roar,
   Their impetus all owe to me.

Chief force of Nature Heaven's great King
   To work His will on Earth employs—
My privilege *greatest* is to bring
   Sweet Hope and Peace, with all their joys.

Man's worship crave I not, nor praise,
   But love ; for, rightly understood,
My mission is his thoughts to raise
   From Nature up to Nature's God.

A Tree Song.

Each season lends to me its special charm—
   The Spring and Summer give me green robes fair,
The Autumn tints me with its colours warm,
   While Winter clothes in white my branches bare.

I canopy the hill sides with my shade,
   O'erarching babbling brook and silent pool;
I hide the squirrels in the woodland glade;
   The shepherd's boy rests 'neath my shelter cool.

To me the wild birds pipe their minstrelsy,
   And build their nests amid my leafy charms:
I rock their cradles to my lullaby,
   And soothe their young in my arboreal arms.

Though firmly rooted in the ground stand I,
    Heavenward I rear my strong-limbed, branching stem :
Thus mine's the Sweetness of the Earth and Sky,
    And mine the Influence that flows from them.

To know my power so subtle dost thou yearn,
    And share the savours that effuse from me ?
This is the lesson thou must con and learn—
    " Live close to Nature and Simplicity."

A Spring Morning at Grange=over=Sands.

This vernal-perfect morn I've climbed
  Yewbarrow's craggy height,
Where now I sit and gaze upon
  A captivating sight.

The turf-clad rock slopes steeply down
  To meads outspreading green,
Where curls the blue smoke from the homes
  Of Grange—fair Morecambe's Queen.

The waters of the Bay beyond
  Are gleaming dazzling-bright,
And sparkling in the sunshine like
  A sea of diamond-light.

Across the waves, which gently break
    Upon the yellow sand,
Uprear the slopes of Arnside Knott
    And the hills of Westmoreland.

How peaceful, beautiful the scene,
    Illumined far and near,
With solar radiance glorified
    Into a vision fair !

O'erhead a speckled throstle pipes,
    A rook flaps slowly by,
A skylark's notes are raining from
    The cloudless azure sky.

Around me wave the grasses long;
    The softly whispering trees
Their branches bare are swaying to
    The bidding of the breeze,

Which fans my forehead aching, hot—
  Its vitalising breath
Infusing life and vigour new,
  Re-establishing my Faith.

Reclining 'neath this sheltering rock,
  Cheered by the sun's warm rays,
My soul responds to Nature's Voice,
  My heart goes out in praise,

Unto the Giver of all good,
  By whose benignant Hand
Such soul-uplifting loveliness
  Bedecks our own dear Land.

Yewbarrow Crag,
  Grange,
  March 6th, 1890

Easter Eve on Yewbarrow Crag, Grange-over-Sands.

Slow fades the splendour of the day,
  And Phœbus' steeds their course have run ;
The landscape, robed in sober grey,
  Is crimsoned by the sinking sun.

The thrush has ceased his evensong,
  The blackbird's throbbing throat now rests ;
And silently on pinions strong
  The crows and curlews seek their nests.

The new-lit lamps of Grange below
  Like glow-worms in the darkness seem ;
The distant lights of Morecambe show,
  And Carnforth's flaring furnace-gleam.

How calm and peaceful is the scene !
  How fragrant sweet the balmy air !
Was hush-time ever more serene ?
  Did prospect ever seem more fair ?

While lingering here it seems to me
  As if a Presence vast, divine,
Were brooding o'er it lovingly,
  Breathing its Spirit into mine.

April 16th, 1892.

A Midsummer Day in Rivington.

How sweet, to-day, to wander through the woods
 And lanes of Rivington, and note the charm
Of flower and bird, of tree and sky and clouds,
 Rejoicing all in Summer's sunshine warm !

Of lilac, wall-flower, apple pink and white,
 The air is fragrant with the odours sweet ;
While buttercups and daisies, colour-bright,
 Be-star the clovered grass beneath our feet.

The trees outspread their leafy screens of green,
 To catch the warmth and brightness of the sun ;
The ferns uncurl their feathery fronds and lean
 Across the brooks which prattle as they run.

The chestnut rears its spires of waxen white,
    Like candles on some giant Christmas tree :
The half-grown corn, swept by the breezes light,
    Is undulating like a grassy sea.

The hawthorn trees, all whitened o'er with flowers,
    Are bending 'neath their wealth of summer snow;
The fountain-like laburnum's dripping showers
    Of gold are mirrored in the lake below,

Across whose bosom swallows skim along,
    On tireless pinions, swift and arrowy ;
While larks pour down their cataract of song
    From out the azure, cloud-flecked, sunny sky.

Beyond the placid lake, empurpled deep,
    The farms, the church, the village nestling lie
Backed by the noble Pike, upsloping steep,
    With crowning Tower clean-cut against the sky.

Within the shadow-dappled woods and glens
    The feathered choristers high revel hold—
The throstles, linnets, chaffinches, and wrens,
    The sable blackbirds with their beaks of gold.

The harsh-voiced corn-crake's monotone is heard,
    The cuckoo shouts his name with glad delight ;
The fledgling crows, taught by the parent bird,
    Make hesitating, first attempts at flight.

The plover utters his sweet, plaintive note,
    And *pee-wit, pee-wit* overhead resounds ;
While from the robin-redbreast's throbbing throat
    Outflows a ripple of melodious sounds.

Adown the slopes the yellow gorse and broom
    Outflame in all their gleaming gorgeousness ;
The woods and fields, with hyacinthine bloom,
    Are azured into perfect loveliness.

The blossom of the mountain-ash bestrews
    The pathway, where, like scattered snow, it lies ;
The rhododendrons flaunt their gaudy hues
    In wealth of florid bloom before our eyes.

The butterflies flit past the blossoming plum,
    Like gaily-tinted, liberated flowers,
And sip the nectar from the apple bloom
    And honeysuckle, all the summer hours.

Around their dams the lambkins skip and bleat ;
    The young calves and the foals sport merrily ;
The luscious new-grown grass the cattle eat,
    Or chew their cud, reclining lazily.

At eve the sun, a glowing, golden shield,
    Behind the hills sinks slowly down to rest,
Illuminating sky and wood and field,
    Like some vast fiery furnace in the West.

So fades this lovely summer-zenith day

    In beauteous Rivington ; and long 'twill be

Ere its sweet influences pass away

    From my responsive heart and memory.

Rivington, near Bolton,
    June 21st, 1894.

A September Evening at Torquay.

As fades the gladsome day I sit alone,
 In sight of ever beautiful Torquay ;
A wave-worn, rocky boulder for my throne,
 Beside the margin of the flowing sea.

Enhaloed in a golden glory-cloud,
 The red September sun has sunk to rest ;
And slowly-gathering gloaming shades enshroud
 The after-glow, now paling in the West.

The daylight, lingering long, seems loth to go,
 As if withheld by some great spirit hand ;
The waters of the bay, inrolling slow,
 Curl o'er and break upon the wrinkled sand.

High overhead a screaming seagull floats
    And oscillates on wide-out-stretching wings ;
While o'er the unruffled sea the white-sailed boats
    Glide with the grace of animated things.

A herald star outshines upon the shore—
    'Tis mighty Jupiter outgleaming bright ;
And soon the azure vault is studded o'er
    With myriad scintillating points of light.

Across the crowded heavens the Milky Way
    Extends its faintly luminous belt of stars ;
While on the glassy bosom of the bay
    There glints a sheen of light from ruddy Mars.

The outlines of the land are picked out by
    The flickering gas lamps rising tier on tier,
Where, like some citadel uptowering high,
    Torquay o'erlooks the starlit waters clear.

How still the air !   The silence how profound !
   The holy, all-pervading peace and calm
Are undisturbed save by the rhythmic sound
   Of mighty Ocean's never-ending psalm.

While gazing on this beauteous scene I seem
   As if transported to some blissful spot,
Where life is one continued happy dream,
   And carking care and trouble enter not.

1893.

Shap Wells.

Familiar from my childhood's days,
A song I'll sing in thy dear praise,
    Sweet, health-restoring spot !
Fair Sanatorium of the North,
Whose beauty and salubrious worth
    Time influences not.

How sweet it is to lie and dream
Beside thy bouldered, peaty stream,
    And to its music list ;
F

As through thy fir-treed wood it speeds,
Meandering from flowery meads
    To mountains wreathed with mist !

Within thy cool, sequestered dells
The foxgloves and the wild blue-bells
    Tempt bee and butterfly ;
While in thy tangled, fragrant glens
The finches and the tiny wrens
    Out-trill their melody.

What joy to tramp thy heathery hills
Bestreaked by straths and foaming rills,
    And breathe thy tonic air !
What gladness on thy heights to stand
And from their vantage ground command
    Thy prospects passing fair !

'Tis mong thy fir woods, hills, and fells

That Nature's great physician dwells—

 Healer of human ills.

Sick mortal, ask'st thou to be cured

Of ailments thou hast long endured ?

 Then haste thee to these hills :

August 15th, 1893.

A Blackpool Sunset.

The evening tide is ebbing peacefully,
Low hanging clouds lie o'er the tranquil sea.
No sound disturbs the silence, save the dirge
Of mighty Ocean and the ceaseless surge
Of white-topped wavelets curling on the sand,
Or breaking gently on the pebbly strand.

The setting sun, slow sinking in the west,
Begilds the low-hung clouds from base to crest;
While from his disc, now flaming fiercely bright,

Shoot radiating spokes of glittering light ;
And through the rifts that rend the cloudy screen
Gleam widening streaks of silver, blue, and green.

More gorgeous grows the picture—changing slow,
Like some sublime phantasmagorial show.

The fleecy cloudlets, dappled o'er the sky,
Are crimsoned as if stained with blood-red dye.

And now the heavens to red and gold are turned,
As if some mighty conflagration burned.

Again a change !   A bank of purple clouds
The dazzling glory of the sun enshrouds.

But soon again he flashes out his light
And, sinking in the sea, is lost to sight.

Another transformation !   Now it seems
As if from out the blazing sky there streams
A cataract of metal, molten hot,
From some gigantic furnace smelting-pot.

The clouds, high towering in the eastern blue,
Are tinted with a blushing roseate hue ;
While north and south the colour pales away
To violet, saffron, heliotrope, dove-grey,
All blended in soft-graded harmony
And mirrored in the gently moving sea.

Slow the celestial colour-splendour fades ;
Too soon " the soft voluptuous opiate shades "
Of eve descend upon the vision bright ;
The darkness closes in, and it is Night.

September 18th, 1891

A Snow Thought.

Scenes that are wondrous fair,
This morn are everywhere :
For snow has fallen in the night,
And robed the slumbering world in white.

On street and roof it lies—
An essence from the skies,
Pure as the angels' feathery down—
Transfiguring the dingy town.

It seems as if, in love,
Our Father from above
His mantle of forgiveness vast
Upon a guilty world had cast.

Alas! that men elect

His mercy to reject!

And trample it beneath their feet,

As snow is trodden in the street.

December 8th, 1889.

A Winter Plaint.

I'm a-weary, weary, weary,
   And my heart is weighted down
With the melancholy dulness
   Of the sombre, grimy town.

For dreary is the Winter
   'Neath our sullen, sunless skies,
And cheerless is the prospect
   That out-spreads before my eyes.

I am longing for the sunshine,
   The songbirds and the flowers,
The brightness and the beauty
   Of the golden summer hours.

Oh, for the freshening breezes
    That sweep o'er hill and fell !
Oh for the balmy zephyrs,
    And the happiness they tell !

Come, haste to burst earth's fetters,
    Soft breath'd, reviving Spring!
To Nature's heart, slow-pulsing,
    Rejuvenescence bring.

Command the grass and flowers
    To clothe the naked land,
The trees to don their raiment,
    The sheathed leaves to expand.

But what are those green bladelets
    Just peeping through the earth ?
They are crocuses and snowdrops,
    Betok'ning vernal birth.

Hurrah !   The Winter's over ;
Spring's breath is in the air ;
And soon the joys of Summer
Will crown the gladsome year.

March, 1895.

When Comes the Merry Spring, O.

When hushed and prostrate Nature lies,

With glassy film spread o'er her eyes,

It seems as if in truth she dies

    By Winter's lethal sting, O.

Through this hibernal, death-like sleep

Her heart its languid throb will keep,

Till summoned by the sun to leap,

    When comes the merry Spring, O.

Refrain—Heigho for Spring, O !

    The gladsome days of Spring, O!

    The sweetest time in all the year

    Is the merry, merry time of Spring, O !

What though the sun be hid from sight,
And darksome clouds obscure his light!
Behind them all he still shines bright—
    A celestial, light-crowned King, O.
His warm, revivifying breath
Will animate cold Nature's wraith,
And put to flight the angel Death,
    When comes the merry Spring, O.

The flowers have crept into the ground,
A silence, cheerless and profound,
In wood and meadow reigns around;
    Sad thoughts our hearts now wring, O.
But Winter, bleak with cold and gloom,
Is destined to receive its doom;
And once again the flowers will bloom
    When comes the merry Spring, O.

The snow-drop's chalice will appear,
And crocus show its golden spear;
The hyacinth its bells will rear,
　　And wreaths of blue will fling, O.
The daffodils the meads will gild,
The cowslips deck the verdant field,
And violets peep 'neath hedges' bield,
　　When comes the merry Spring, O.

Gold buttercups and daisies white
The greening earth will then bedight,
And woodland choirs, with glad delight,
　　Their hymns of praise will sing, O.
The trees, now leafless, stark and bare,
Like grim, gaunt spectres standing there,
Their robes of green again will wear,
　　When comes the merry Spring, O.

The throstle's joyous roundelay
Will echo through the livelong day ;
The soaring lark, with carols gay,
    Will heaven's high arches ring, O.
When wintry clouds of grief and pain
Make cold our hearts, let Hope sustain
Us, that they too will know again
    The joy and warmth of Spring, O.

February, 1890.

To Annan Water.—*A Song.*

Let others chant praises to streams of renown—
   " Sweet Afton," the Wye, or the Shannon—
      But my song shall be
      In honour of thee,
My own, well-beloved River Annan !
Pellucid thy waters, and smoothly they glide,
   Meand'ring through meadow and lea ;
      Their cradle the rills
      From Moffat's steep hills,
Their grave Solway's swift-flowing sea.

Refrain—   Thou dear Annan Water!

Thou sweet Annan Water!

The fairest of Earth's charming streams;

Nothing shall ever

My heart from thee sever,

Or thy loved image blot from my dreams.

Thrice blessèd the childhood companioned by

thee,

And precious the mem'ries that tell

Of happy days past—

Too happy to last !—

That hold us life-long in their spell :

So tenderly close do the years of our youth

Round the heart of our manhood entwine ;

And fond thoughts of joys

That are shared by all boys

Are treasured in memory's shrine.

G

How gladsome those days in thy flowery meads,

　　Where the daisies and buttercups grow ;

　　　　Where forget-me-not's blue

　　　　Rivals heaven's own hue,

　　And the golden-eyed primroses blow !

And gleesome those romps by thine emerald banks,

　　Where we gathered the nodding blue bells !

　　　　What frolics were ours,

　　　　'Mong the rainbow-hued flowers

That dapple thy verdurous dells !

What pleasure to bathe in thy crystalline pools ;

　　In thy murmuring shallows to wade,

　　　　Where the cows seek retreat

　　　　From the summer sun's heat,

　　Or recline 'neath the trees' leafy shade !

What heart-stirring joy, when Jack Frost ruled
　　supreme,

On thy ice-fettered surface to slide ;

   While the curling-stones roar

   'Mid the shouts of the " core,"

And the skaters so gracefully glide !

In thy woods we have searched out the birds'

   mossy nests;

  We have fished in thy slow-ebbing tide ;

   We have hunted the otter

   In thy deep, glassy water,

And sailed o'er thine estuary wide.

Ne'er can we forget the old gambols and games

  Which childhood beatify ever ;

   The " bools," " peeries," kites,

   And the thousand delights

Of *thy* boys, my beautiful River.

Thy fields are aye greenest, thy sunshine's aye
　　brightest ;
　The vault of thy wide-arching dome
　　　Is clearest and bluest ;
　　　Thy friends are the truest,
　And thy name is suggestive of Home—
The heart's House of Refuge, its Sanctuary blest.
　Where'er 'tis my fortune to roam,
　　　'Mid scenes that are rarest,
　　　The sweetest and fairest
　Is Annan, dear Annan, my HOME !

A Sunset Hour at Annan.

———

'Tis gloaming time ; the sun from sight has gone ;
By Annan Waterside I sit, alone,
As fades the summer day, calm and serene,
And note the charm and beauty of the scene.

Across the Holm the sky is all aglow
With sunset-glory colour, changing slow
From crimson-deep to silver, blue, and gold—
Like some sky panorama vast unrolled.

One solitary star shines diamond-bright,
Amidst the deepening afterglow of light

Which in the o'erarching zenith pales away
To amber, amethyst, and softest grey.

Behind is Annan, bathed in rosy light,
Its buildings red upclimbing o'er the height
Where once the valiant Bruce's fortress frowned,
And every furlong marks historic ground.

The grand old Bridge which spans the noble stream,
The houses glowing in the sunset's gleam,
The Town Hall spire upstanding high in air,
Are mirrored in the River's bosom fair.

The swallows dart and scream, the seagulls float
Above the dark tree masses of the Moat;
A homing pewitt silhouettes the sky
And breaks the silence with its plaintive cry.

How fair, how dear, the scene before my eyes!

How eloquent of happy memories,

And recollections sweet of boyhood's days,

Which death alone can from my heart erase!

Near the " Whin Bush."
    July 12th, 1895.

A Summer Song.

A song let me sing of the halcyon days,
Of summer time joyous and sweet;
When, from morning till night,
I am filled with delight,
In this lovely Arcadian retreat.
The golden sun in the glory of noon
Floods the world with his life-giving rays,
And warms the earth's great
Throbbing heart, now elate
With pæans and anthems of praise;

Chorus.—Hurrah for the summer!
The glorious summer!
When Nature is radiant and gay;

The birds in the bowers,

The trees and the flowers,

Rejoice in the glad summer's day.

The larks soaring high in the heavenly blue

Trill forth their matins of praise;

The thrushes and wrens

In the copses and glens

Are merrily chanting their lays.

The robins and chaffinches hid 'mong the trees

Have joined the aerial choir,

And all the day long

Pour forth the sweet song

Which the bright days of summer inspire.

The roses are wooing the scent-laden breeze

From the sweet honeysuckle that blows;

And from fragrant hawthorn,

To the ripening corn

On the slopes of the uplands that grows,

The gossamer butterflies flit to and fro,

Like wingèd and vivified flowers,

And from chalices bright

Sip honeyed delight,

Through the beautiful sunshiny hours.

The tender-eyed kine, knee-deep in the mead,

Crop the herbage so juicy and sweet ;

While the bees hum and hover

'Mong the red and white clover,

And the nectar-filled cups at our feet.

The long meadow grass, now mellow and ripe,

Is falling beneath the sharp scythe,

As, with rhythmical sweep,

The mowers time keep,

To the song they are singing so blythe.

Let us hie to the woods, where the sun visions dance

    Round the foxgloves like elfins of light,

        And reclining at ease,

        'Neath the shade of the trees,

    We shall " loafe and our souls we'll invite."

If we're friends with the birds and the starry wild

    flowers,

    They will whisper this message divine :—

        " We are tokens of love,

        From Our Father above,

    Sent to tell of His Purpose benign."

Dormont Grange, near Annan.
    June, 1889.

A Spring Day at Annan.

I.

What joy it is to see again,
  The little town I love so well!
To look upon the dear old home
  Where my belovèd kinsfolk dwell!

To wander up and down the house,
  And through the garden, now abloom
With apple blossom pink and white,
  With cherry, strawberry, and plum!

To hear the old familiar songs
  Of "blackie," "yallow yoit," and thrush,
Trilled forth in joyous ecstasy
  From break of day till evening's hush!

To saunter by the grassy banks
  Of Annan Water, and to gaze
On scenes endeared by memories
  Of childhood's, boyhood's happy days—

The Violetbank, the Watermill,
  Old Milnbie Quarry and the Howes,
The Milnfield Wood, the Quay, the Dam,
  The Well, the Waterfoot, Hayknowes;

The Battery Brae, the Quartercake,
  The Moat with its enclosing wall,
The Caul, the Bankin' and the Brig—
  What memories sweet these names recall!

What merry sports and games were ours
  When we were laddies at the school!—
The cricketing upon the Merse,
  The fishing near the old Howes Pool!

What fun we had at " dookin'-time !"
  What gleesome scampers, hand in hand,
By Whinnyrigg to Seafield beach
  To bathe, or race upon the sand !

Then the delights of Annan Fair !
  And how we revelled in its joys—
The sweeties, Cheap Jacks, Jimmy Dyer,
  The shows, the fairin's, and the toys !

No " Caledonian Hunters " then,
  Nor switchback railways driven by steam ;
But wooden steeds propelled by boys,
  Whose " free-ride " hopes oft proved a dream.

And what a treat to see a launch—
  To be aboard the ship, and feel
Her gliding down the slippery ways,
  To cleave the water with her keel ;

To hear the shouts and loud hurrahs
    That issue from a thousand throats,
As through the tide she ploughs her way,
    And o'er its surface proudly floats!

II.

Oft as I've roved my River's banks,
    By verdant wood and sunny brae,
Methinks they never seemed more fair,
    More sweetly charming, than to-day.

The balmy air is perfumed with
    The fragrance of the time of Spring,
Which in the earth new life inspires,
    And clothes with beauty everything.

The tender blades of sprouting corn
    Begreen the brown, parturient earth;

And Nature universal feels
   The travail-throes of vernal birth.

The bud its scaly leaf-case splits,
   The waking floweret opes its eye,
The caterpillar issues from
   Its chrysalis—a butterfly.

The cuckoo loud repeats his name,
   The swallows scream with voices shrill,
The wee lambs round their mothers play,
   The young calves browse upon the hill.

The rooks, perched on their rude-made nests
   High in the slowly leafing trees,
Are cawing to their half-fledged broods
   Rocked gently by the passing breeze.

The daisy stars the greening Holm ;
   At Galabank the primrose shows

Its eye of gold; while silently
 The beauteous River onward flows.

Dear Annan ! Magnet of my heart !
 What potent influence dost thou wield !
What sacred ties unite me to
 Thy every street, and wood, and field !

Or east or west, or north or south,
 Where'er thy sons or daughters roam,
They never, never can forget
 That thou, dear Annan, art their HOME.

May, 1891.

H

Edward Irving.

No highly-born patrician, thou ;
No coronet adorns thy brow ;
A tanner's son, of humble birth,
Thy passport is not wealth, but worth.

Boyhood friend of Clapperton—
Annan's bold, adventurous son ;
Manhood friend of Carlyle, who
Called thee " generous, noble, true."

True to the Faith thou didst believe ;
True to the Light thou didst receive ;
True to thy Church, despite the strife
Which bittered thy heroic life.

Alas ! that by its narrow creeds
The Church thou lovedst so must needs
Expel thee from its cleric fold—
Its dogma strict thou couldst not hold.

Thy errors, which we deep deplore,
Constrain us but to love thee more,
And honour thy staunch faithfulness—
Thy ministry of righteousness.

Dauntless follower of thy Lord,
Seeing in His living word
Light and guidance definite—
Upholding it with all thy might.

Preacher, prophet, martyr, saint ;
Life untouched by slander's taint ;
Immortal Irving ! thy renown
Enhaloes our beloved town.

Honouring thee, thy townsmen pay

Honour to themselves to-day ;

And that Annan loves thee well,

Let its sculptured marble tell.

Sung by the Choir at the unveiling of the Irving
Statue, at Annan, August 4th, 1892.

OTHER SONGS AND VERSES.

My Preference.

———

I love the joyous sunshine,
  The air, the trees, the flowers ;
I love to hear the songbirds
  Carol in leafy bowers.

I love the sweeping landscapes ;
  The hills, the lakes, the sea,
The sky and sailing cloudlets
  Have each a charm for me.

I love to watch the children
  As out of school they troop ;
I love to watch them playing
  With skipping-rope and hoop.

MUSA MEDICA.

I love the throbbing movement
  And bustle of the street,
The thronging of the people,
  The clank of horses' feet.

I love to sit and ponder
  In some secluded nook,
My silent, sole companion,
  An interesting book.

But best of all my heart loves
  Communion with the friends
Whose fealty and affection
  I am *sure* of, till life ends.

True to the Core.

Some wish for Learning and place 'mong the wise,

Others on Wealth look with covetous eyes ;

But a Treasure more precious than Riches or Lore

Is a friend who is loyal and true to the core.

> *Refrain.*—True to the core, true to the core,
>
> A friend who is loyal and true to the core.

Loyal to all that is noblest and best

In man or in woman, when put to the test ;

Loving his fellows, or wealthy or poor,

With a heart that is loyal and true to the core.

> True to the core, &c.

Loyal to Manliness, Honour, and Right ;
For the weak and defenceless aye ready to fight
Scornful of everything good men abhor,
Brimful of sympathy, true to the core.

   True to the core, &c.

Loyal to Truth, regardless of creeds,
Daring to follow wherever it leads ;
Nobly courageous men's scorn to ignore,
True to his Better Self, true to the core.

   True to the core, &c.

Our pleasures are doubled when shared by a friend,
A charm to each joy does his company lend ;
In sorrow no balm for the heart wounded sore,
Can soothe like the friend who is true to the core.

   True to the core, &c.

May all friends whose hearts are loving and leal
Be " grappled together with strong hooks of steel " !
And hand in hand stand up the whole world before,
As Brothers and Comrades all, true to the core.

Refrain.—True to the core, true to the core,

As Brothers and Comrades all, true to
the core.

At Wordsworth's Grave.

(A true incident.)

One summer eve, alone, I stood
    In Grasmere's peaceful, green churchyard,
In silent, meditative mood,
    Beside the grave of Nature's bard.

Above the stone a sheltering yew
    Its graceful, feathery branches spread,
A flowering chestnut-tree upthrew
    Its spires of milk-white bloom o'erhead.

A throstle and a blackbird sang
    Their evensongs upon the trees ;
The cuckoo's " twofold shout " outrang
    And echoed through the scented breeze,

Which sighed among the rustling leaves,
   Whispering sweet music in mine ear ;
While swallows twittered on the eaves,
   Or skimmed the river, murmuring near.

The mist-capped mountains stood around
   Like giants huge of ghostly mien,
Guarding the sacred burial ground,
   Lending enchantment to the scene.

There came a little pilgrim maid ;
   " Her hair was thick with many a curl " ;
She was " only eight years old," she said—
   A sweetly pretty, blue-eyed girl.

I asked her why she had come there ;
   She looked at me so calmly brave,
And answered, with a childish air—
   " To visit Mr. Wordsworth's grave."

" And who was Mr. Wordsworth, child ? "
   I fear she thought me very dull,
As she replied, and sweetly smiled—
   " He wrote our poetry at school."

"Which poem do you like the best ? "
   " Oh, I like ' We are Seven,' " said she ;
And, upon being gently pressed,
   She said the verses o'er to me.

As fast the shades of twilight fell
   Upon those green-grassed mounds of death,
And as I heard the words which tell
   Of childhood's simple, trustful faith,

Methought the poet's spirit near
   Was hovering in the waning light ;
And this its message—" Have no fear !
   Thy loved ones are but gone from sight."

A Song for Burns's Birthday,

There is a Land, a braw, braw Land,
   Wi' lochs, and glens, and a' that,
Where spates roar doon frae mountains grand,
   And bluebells nod, and a' that.
      For a' that, and a' that,
         For beauty rare and a' that,
         Auld Scotland aye can haud her ain
            'Mang foreign lands, and a' that.

They tell o' countries vast and fair,
   Wi' azure skies, and a' that,
Where soft and balmy is the air,
   And life's a dream, and a' that.

For a' that, and a' that,
    Their orange groves, and a' that,
    The banks and braes o' Scotia still
    Are dearer far than a' that.

Where'er her sons and dochters gae,
    Tae distant climes, and a' that,
Their herts are aye fast anchored tae
    Their ain wee Land, for a' that.
    For a' that, and a' that
        Their honours, wealth, and a' that,
    They never, never can forget
    That Scotland's *hame*, for a' that.

In her prood galaxy ae name
    Shines solar-bricht, and a' that—
'Tis Burns, wha's memory and fame
    We toast this nicht, and a' that.

For a' that, and a' that,

For hertsome sangs, and a' that,

'Mang poets a' the warld ower,

He bears the gree, and a' that.

Scotland's immortal Peasant Bard !

We loo thee weel, and a' that ;

And our affection warm is shared

By England's sons, and a' that.

For a' that, and a' that,

Though sundered far, an a' that,

A warld-wide throng doth thee acclaim

Great King-o'-herts, and a' that.

Sung at the Burns' Anniversary,
Bolton, January 25th, 1896.

I

Burns.

This nicht the hert o' Scotland turns
Wi' fond affection tae her Burns ;
The nicht on which "the Januar' wun
Blew hansel in " on her great son.

In him a' Scotia's sons rejoice,
For in him Scotland fand her voice ;
A voice wi' accents sweet that sings
O' humble folks and common things—

The simple annals o' the poor
In lowly cot on glen or moor ;
The timorous mouse, the hunted hare,.
The "crimson-tippèd " daisy fair.

Hoo dear tae us ilk theme and scene!
His " Cottar " and his " Halloween,"
The bogles' doin's i' the mirk,
By " Alloway's auld haunted Kirk "!

What sweetness in his love sangs dwells!
And hoo the hert wi' gladness swells,
As sings he " Highland Mary's " praise,
Or tells o' " Doon's fair banks and braes "!

For humour, wut, and doonricht fun,
Oor Robin is surpassed by none;
And wha withoot a lauch can hear
The tale o' " Tam o' Shanter's mear? "

His satire's keen, but no' unkind,
On folks that werna tae his mind;
And Cant's been seldom lashed sae sair
As in his " Holy Wullie's prayer."

What noble thochts oor spirits fan
When Robin sings " A man's a man " !
And when did poet chant a lay
Mair stirrin' than his " Scots wha hae "?

What land or clime may Scotsmen claim,
The sang that minds them o' their hame,
And a' their herts and hands can twine,
Is Burns's deathless " Auld Lang Syne."

Great Magnet o' the North, wha's power
Draws Scotland's sons the warld ower !
To thee we love and homage bring,
And hail thee Scotia's Poet-king !

Read at the Burns' Anniversary,
Bolton, January 25th, 1895.

A Cycle Song.

Let others sing loudly of pastimes and joys
Endeared to the hearts of men, maidens, and boys;
My ditty shall be of the pleasures I feel
When mounted secure on my dearly-loved Wheel.

Chorus:

Hurrah for the Cycle, swift, trusty, and strong!
May it daily win lovers and stay with us long!
Good luck let us wish to the Courser of steel,
And Health and Long Life to the Men of the Wheel!

It carries me swiftly and safely along,
Away from the town with its noise and its throng;

Away from the stifling and smoke-laden air,
To the life-giving breezes and rural scenes fair.

  Chorus.—Hurrah for the Cycle, &c.

The whole world is mine to wander at will ;
For me are the glories of valley and hill ;
The larks in the sky and the flowers on the lea
Shed sweetness and beauty for Cycle and me.

  Chorus.—Hurrah for the Cycle, &c.

When tired of the city, its clamour and strife,
My Pegasus bears me to newness of life ;
And nought can relieve the sad heart of its load
Of worry and care, like a " spin " on the road.

  Chorus.—Hurrah for the Cycle, &c.

Let the rich in their coaches and carriages roll,
My Cycle is better by far than them all ;

The Wheel of Dame Fortune to them may bring
    Wealth,
But my flying Wheel is the Wheel of Good Health.

Chorus:

Hurrah for the Cycle, swift, trusty, and strong!
May it daily win lovers and stay with us long!
Good luck let us wish to the Courser of steel,
And Health and Long Life to the Men of the Wheel!

July 17th, 1895.

A Curling Ditty.

———

'Mang Scotia's sports and pastimes a',
Dear tae her sons, in cot or ha',
There's nane that's worthy o' the name
Can match the Royal Curlin' Game.

* * *

When King Frost lays his iron hand
Upon the bare and silent land,
The Bolton chiels turn oot tae play,
Wi' faces eager for the fray.

At Ladybrig pond they a' meet
And yin anither kindly greet ;
Stanes, brooms, and cramps are carried oot
Frae the auld weather-beaten hut.

In order, on the ice they're laid,
The rinks are formed, the skips are made,
And soon aroon' the new-ringed tee
Begins the freen'ly rivalry.

See hoo they rax and strain tae send
The "channel stanes" frae end tae end !
And hoo each strives, wi' micht and main,
His rink's supremacy tae gain !

What language strange breaks on the ear !
Hoo foreign-like it soon's, and queer !
What means sic mystic words as these—
"Inwicks," "shots," "pat-lids," and "tees"?

Cries yin—"Joost break an egg on this,
And tak' ye care ye dinna miss !"
" Losh, man, ye canna curl a bit—
That wad ha' smashed a cocoa nit !"

" Haud aff, haud aff, lads !" cries anither ;

" Oh, he's awa' wi't a'thegither !"

" Noo, Peter, dinna you be hard,

Draw tae my broom and mind the guard."

" Div ye see this, Ben ? " next says ane—

" It's second cast and it's their stane ;

Joost come up canny—chap and lie ;

Oh, bring him on !   Noo let him die !"

" Ye see this, John ?   Weel, leave't alane ;

I want ye joost tae raise this stane ;

It's in the ring—ye'll no' be short !

Oh, man, ye're roarin' through the port ! "

" Come, Sandie, draw the port—tee len'th ;

Played !   But I doot ye haena' stren'th :

Oh, soop him up, lads, soop ; and fegs !

He'll be a coonter, if he's legs."

Again a skip cries—"Guard this, Mac!
It's on the tee, sae lie weel back."
" Noo, Egbert, can ye rub the guard,
Or lift this ither yin a yard ? "

"Come, Doctor, ye maun tak' yer will
O' thae twa paitricks—shew's yer skill :
Oh, loaven enty, he's awa',
And ta'en oor best stane tae the snaw !"

" Noo, George, draw here—we finger twirl :
I like ye weel, man—that's the curl ;
Oh it's a great yin, there's nae doot ;
Ne'er a coo, lads !   That's the shot !"

" Cloor this yin, Bob, upon the lug,
And, mind, the ice is gettin' drug :
Ye're wabblin', man, but weel laid on :
Played like a book! Weel dune, weel dune!"

" Noo, Minister, they're lyin' fower;
Sae ye maun fire, wi' a' yer power :
Hooray, hooray !   They're oot, they're oot !
I kent the Minister could do't."

" Oh, Tam, oh, Tam, ye lazy dog !
Ye want mair brose—ye're near a hog ;
Sic play wad gar a body sweer ;
Here, laddie, bring some mair warm beer !"

" Noo, Davie, ye maun try and draw—
We've naething in the hoose ava !"
" Get haud o' him !   Soop weel !   Hooray !
Ye're shot, Dave !   That's the way tae play !"

   *   *   *

But wha can a' their cantrips tell ?
And hoo they skrech, and loup, and yell ?
And hoo they praise, and hoo they flyte ?
As if they had a' gane clean gyte.

   *   *   *

Thus does the gleesome game gang on,

Until the slowly westerin' sun

Embathes the snaw upon the hills,

And earth and sky wi' glory fills.

As slow the shades of eve descend,

The Merry Curlers hameward wend

Their way ; and that nicht, at the " Swan,"

They fecht their battles ower again.

Read at the Annual Dinner of the Bolton Branch of the Royal
Caledonian Curling Club, December 11th, 1895.

Scotia; or, Both Sides.

***

A DIALOGUE

BETWEEN

Donald—A Highland Collie,

AND

Jack—An English Terrier.

Donald—Scotland!   Theme o' poets' lays!
    Mine be it tae sing thy praise ;
    And tae tell o' things that move
    Scotsmen a' tae pride and love.

Jack— Mine be it to criticise,
    And to look with English eyes
    On the other side of things,
    While our good friend Donald sings.

Donald—Land o' mountains, falls and torrents,
　　　　Lochs and glens o' beauty rare ;
　　　　Grassy meadows, spreading forests,
　　　　Sunny braes and landscapes fair.

Jack—　Land of fog and mist and rain,
　　　　Ghillies, tourists, landlords, bills ;
　　　　Tartans, dirks, and filleybegs,
　　　　Shebeens and illicit stills.

Donald—Land o' bluebells, purple heather,
　　　　Linns and crags and bosky glens,
　　　　Sea-washed cliffs and massive boulders,
　　　　Murmuring rills and frowning Bens.

Jack—　Land of hotch-potch, brose, and "kebbucks,"
　　　　Bannocks, haggis, kale, and parritch ;
　　　　Land of golfing, curling, shinty,
　　　　Grouse and "paitricks," prayers and
　　　　"carritch."

Donald—Land o' scholars, poets, heroes,

        Wha hae left an honoured name,

        Haloing the name o' Scotland

        Wi' the glory o' their fame.

Jack—   Land of " fechtin' " chiefs and clansmen—

        Scheming rogues of deepest dye ;

        Land of kilted " heelan' teevils,"

        Border raiders, lifted " kye."

Donald—Land o' stalwart sons and dochters,

        Canty chiels and denty queans,

        Reels and hoolicans and bagpipes,

        Hogmanays and halloweens.

Jack—   Land of wizards, brownies, witches ;

        " Unco gude " and pious folks ;

        " Usquebae," and saintly elders,

        Thistles, scones, and " bubbly jocks."

Donald—Land o' preachers, saints, and martyrs—

    Heroes braver earth ne'er trod—

Covenanters, and defenders

    O' their Country and their God.

Jack—   Land of kirks and psalms and sermons;

    " Holy Wullies "—on the Sunday—

But who have no hesitation

    Their best friend to cheat on Monday.

Donald—Land o' schools and education ;

    Land wha's sons, frae South and North,

Wandering a' the warld ower

    Prove themselves o' sterling worth.

Jack—   Land of " canny," saving bodies,

    " Bawbees," " saxpences," and " caddies ";

Land of " sneeshin'," " spluchens," " spel-

    drins,"

    " Glesca' magistrates " and " haddies."

K

Donald—Land o' Freedom which doth ever
      Foreign domination spurn;
    Land wha's foes hae no' forgotten
      Robert Bruce and Bannockburn.

Jack—   Land that broke its faith with Edward
      When a truce of peace was sealed;
    Land whose sons have not forgotten
      English pluck and Flodden Field.

Donald—Land historic, land romantic,
      Land o' Wallace, Burns, and Scott;
    Land wha's memory time and distance
      Frae oor herts eraseth not.

Jack—   Land whose sons are aye declaring
      They adore each hill and " stane,"
    But who take care, when they leave it,
      Never to go back again.

Baby Boy.

Baby Boy,
Mother's joy,
Father's hope and pride ;
Where got you
Eyes so blue,
Opening so wide ?

Sunny curls,
Teeth like pearls,
Cheeks red as a rose ;
Soft pink skin,
Dimpled chin,
Dainty little nose.

Winsome wiles,
Happy smiles,
Sometimes mixed with tears ;
Face o'ercast,
Cloud soon past,
Once again it clears.

Prattling talk,
Toddling walk,
Up and down the house ;
In and out,
Round about ;
Scampering little mouse.

Romp and play
All the day,
Wee feet seldom rest ;
Till at night
Baby bright
Curls up in his nest.

A Christmas Hymn.

This morn we celebrate His birth
Whose herald-word was " Peace on Earth,'
And thanks accord the Lord of Heaven
For blessings rich and varied given :—

For life, for health, for kinsfolk dear,
For home and for our friends sincere ;
For tender, sweet domestic joys
With partners, parents, girls, and boys.

For glad re-unions, heart with heart,
And all the pleasure they impart ;
For all the happy days we've known ;
For all the kindness to us shewn.

For goodness, love, and charity ;
Material prosperity ;
For vital sunlight, freshening shower ;
For leaf and fruit, for bird and flower.

For season's shows, for Nature's stores,
Which she in rich profusion pours :
For all to us vouchsafed of good
Let us praise Him with gratitude.

And while we journey on our way,
Be this our prayer from day to day :—
For hearts unselfish, gentle, kind ;
For sympathy with all mankind.

For strength temptation fierce to fight ;
For firm resolve to do the right ;
For courage troublous times to face ;
For steadfastness to run life's race.

For will and power to help the oppressed ;
To succour all who are distressed ;
To do our duty in our work,
And difficulties ne'er to shirk.

To know the happiness that lies
In service and self-sacrifice ;
To quit ourselves in all we do,
Like honest, upright men, and true.

And when the beckoning angels come
To bear us to Our Father's Home—
The conflict o'er, the victory won—
May we receive the Lord's " Well done!"

Christmas, 1890.

www.ingramcontent.com/pod-product-compliance
Lightning Source LLC
Chambersburg PA
CBHW021135020726
47500CB00003B/1088